W9-BLN-859

Weekly Reader Books presents

The ALLIGATOR and His UNCLE TOOTH

A Novel of the Sea

by Geoffrey Hayes

HARPER & ROW, PUBLISHERS
New York, Hagerstown, San Francisco, London

This book is a presentation of
Weekly Reader Books.
Weekly Reader Books offers
book clubs for children from
preschool to young adulthood. All
quality hardcover books are selected
by a distinguished Weekly Reader
Selection Board.

For further information write to:
Weekly Reader Books
1250 Fairwood Ave.
Columbus, Ohio 43216

The Alligator and His Uncle Tooth
Copyright © 1977 by Geoffrey Hayes
All rights reserved. No part of this book may be used or
reproduced in any manner whatsoever without written
permission except in the case of brief quotations embodied
in critical articles and reviews. Printed in the United
States of America. For information address Harper & Row,
Publishers, Inc., 10 East 53rd Street, New York, N.Y. 10022.
Published simultaneously in Canada by Fitzhenry & Whiteside
Limited, Toronto.

Library of Congress Cataloging in Publication Data
Hayes, Geoffrey.
    The alligator and his Uncle Tooth.

    SUMMARY: A shy young alligator meets his
Uncle Tooth, a crusty ex-sea captain, who tells him
of his many adventures at sea.
    [1. Alligators—Fiction. 2. Sea stories] I. Title.
PZ7.H31455Al   [Fic]   76-21387
ISBN 0-06-022264-6
ISBN 0-06-022265-4 lib. bdg.

Designed by Kohar Alexanian

for Rory

Contents

The
ALLIGATOR
and His
UNCLE TOOTH

How Corduroy
Met Uncle Tooth

Once upon a time, there was a house in the hills full of alligators. Uncles, aunts, and cousins, mammas, papas, and children—all lived together in the same house. It was crowded and noisy, but the alligators didn't seem to mind.

They planted vegetable gardens, built kites, made delicious soups, knit sweaters, and gave parties on the lawn. Only when it rained and everyone had to stay indoors did things become really uncomfortable.

This story is about the youngest and smallest alligator, whose name was Corduroy. Because he was forever getting stepped on, shoved aside, or simply ignored, he was not at all happy with life in the Alligator House.

Corduroy spent most of his time alone, either in his room upstairs (which he shared with four other alligator children) or wandering through the hills. He loved the pine forest behind his home, standing strong and silent through every season. When the trees were hung with snow or covered by fog or moved by wind, Corduroy watched them, and it was like poetry.

He loved the contrast of the bright sun shining on the

lawn of the Alligator House and the shadowed coolness of the forest.

Best of all, he loved the little streams that ran rapidly down the hills to the mysterious sea. He had never seen the sea. He wondered what it looked like and what lay beyond it.

"Here we do the same things day after day," he thought. "Why can't life be different and exciting?"

But whenever Corduroy tried talking to the other alligators about this, they only gave him funny looks, or shook their heads and walked away. "It's a comfortable life," one old alligator explained. "Why change it?"

"I guess I'm just different," thought Corduroy sadly. "Well, when I grow up, I intend to leave this place and do something terrific. No knitting sweaters for me!"

Still, life went on the same.

Then, when he was six years old, Corduroy was sent to live with an aunt of his named Hick, who owned a stationery shop in a nearby fishing village. Auntie Hick needed someone to run errands for her, help keep things in order, and provide her with a bit of companionship. None of the other alligators could be bothered, but Corduroy was delighted to go. It would give him a chance to see the ocean and to do something different.

So he packed his belongings in a carpetbag and set off down the wide dirt road. It was only half a day's journey, but it was farther than Corduroy had ever been, and he walked along observing the countryside and thinking happy thoughts.

Late that afternoon, rounding a bend in the road, he came upon the fishing village. The sky loomed over the seashore, as blue as it was endless, and the ocean seemed endless too—a flat, moving field of green water crested with white foam. Corduroy wanted to go down and touch it to make certain it was real.

The village itself was small, just a huddle of houses with narrow winding streets. Auntie Hick's shop stood squeezed between two larger buildings at the end of Tuna Street. It was clean and white as a bone, trimmed

in green, and MISS HICK'S STATIONERY & CON-
FECTIONS was printed over the door in neat black
letters.

Auntie Hick was not nearly as nice as her shop. She
was a tall, withered old alligator who hobbled as
though she had springs on her feet, keeping her paws
close to her sides. She peered at Corduroy through tiny
eyeglasses.

"You're rather scrawny, aren't you?" she said when
she first saw him. Before he could answer, she added,

"Well, come upstairs and I'll show you where you're to sleep."

Corduroy followed her up a winding staircase to a small apartment above the shop. It contained only a sitting room, a kitchen, and Auntie Hick's bedroom, but there was a curtained alcove off the hall with a cot for Corduroy.

"Well," said Auntie Hick, "what do you think?"

"Uh, it's all right," he said.

"Good! Now listen, I have trouble with my nerves, so I won't tolerate any nonsense. You do what I tell you. In your free time you may play where you like, only don't get into any mischief that will disgrace me, or I'll send you back home in half a jiffy!"

As the days passed, Corduroy adapted to his new life rather easily. As long as he did his chores and stayed out of Auntie Hick's way, she did not criticize him too severely.

In the evenings she stayed in the sitting room with the pomegranate wallpaper, reading detective novels, drinking tea spiced with peppermint, or knitting mufflers. She rarely spoke to Corduroy.

He stayed on his bed and wrote in a ledger book from the Five and Dime all the things he wanted to do.

In the daytime when his work was done, Corduroy went exploring in the village or through the surrounding hills. But most of all, he played on the beach. He sank into the deep sand, scooped up pawfuls of it, and threw them over his head. He skipped down to the shoreline where the sand was moist and dark, and as he ran, he left a trail of paw impressions behind him. The sea roared as it swept onto the beach, sending up showers of salty mist that tingled Corduroy's nose. He breathed in the ocean smell. How untamed it was! How alive!

As he sat there watching it, the sea foam rolling on the waves looked like delicate clouds; and the clouds in the sky looked like flower blossoms; and the sky moved like a song. "Poetry!" thought Corduroy.

He dug for clams or hunted for crustaceans and sea urchins. He even found a few starfish and curved, hollow shells. When he held a shell to his ear, Corduroy thought how odd that a little bit of the sea had been left inside—only the echo part.

One day, when the tide went out, it left a number of curious objects scattered behind on the sand: bottles, a jellyfish, some seaweed, an inner tube, tin cans, and several pieces of black, twisted driftwood. Corduroy was so excited, he wandered farther down the coast than he had ever gone before. He had collected an armful of stuff and was ready to start back, when he noticed a foggy spot over at the end of the beach. There the breakers crashed onto tall, dark rocks; and high,

high upon one of the rocks, Corduroy could see the shadow of an alligator. He was all alone against the sky. And he was fishing.

"That's strange," thought Corduroy. "Who would possibly want to fish down there where it's cold and damp?"

Later, as he was sweeping out the shop, his thoughts returned to that lone alligator on the rocks. He wondered who it could be. But then Auntie Hick came in with a list of supplies she needed from the market, so Corduroy went to get them. He forgot all about the strange alligator until a week later. As he was heading downstairs into the stationery shop, he heard Auntie Hick say, "And don't hang around here, you old tramp. Stay on the beach where you belong!"

Then a gruff voice said, "I only wanted to buy some sweets, you old shark!" The front door slammed, and there was a strong odor of tobacco.

"Who was that?" asked Corduroy, coming into the room.

Auntie Hick looked angry. "No one important . . . just a brother of mine named Tooth!" She began absently to straighten some shelves behind her.

"Brother?" said Corduroy. "Then he's my uncle?"

Coming out from behind the counter, Auntie Hick shook her paw at Corduroy. "Listen, I said it's nobody! He's a disgrace to the family name, leaving a comfortable business to go off to sea when he wasn't more than a lad!"

She sat down on a stool, pushed up her sleeves, and

9

dabbed her brow with a pocket-handkerchief. Corduroy could tell she was very upset. "Our family used to own the Five and Dime," said Auntie Hick. "Us children were to take it over when Father retired. We were each to have a share in running it—but no, Tooth wasn't content to lead a respectable life . . . had to go off seeking adventure. Humph! That left your mother and me. We managed the shop quite well without Tooth. But then your mother got married and went to live in the Alligator House. It was too much work for me to run that place alone, so eventually I had to sell it. With the money I made, I was able to buy this stationery shop. But business is slow . . . the customers are uninteresting . . . it's not the same."

Auntie Hick paused for a long while, and Corduroy was afraid to say anything. Then she went on, "When his career as a sea captain was over, Tooth moved back here. He lives in a rotted shack way at the end of the beach. Doesn't want to talk with anyone. Won't even get a job. He just goes fishing every day and sells what he catches. A fine life! He's looney if you ask me. I don't want to hear any more about him or my nerves are going to act up!"

Auntie Hick rose and bustled off to the back room. Corduroy hurried to the door, opened it, and looked down the street, but it was empty.

"An ex-sea captain! That must be the person I saw fishing on the rocks last week!" he thought. "What adventures he must have lived! And to think he is a relative! He doesn't sound looney to me. Maybe he can

tell me what lies beyond the sea."

The next day, Corduroy couldn't do his chores fast enough. When his work was finished, he grabbed his cap and hurried down to the end of the beach. He reached the foggy spot, and the air became cold and wet. On the rocks about him, gulls perched and waddled and screamed; above him, they slid in wide circles through the sky. Among the gulls sat an old alligator with black, wrinkled eyes and tufts of white hair growing out of the sides of his head. He was wearing a pea coat and a seaman's cap.

11

He seemed startled when he noticed Corduroy looking up at him. "Who are you?" he asked in an annoyed
voice. "And what do you want?"

Corduroy spoke up briskly. "Are you Uncle Tooth,
the sea captain?"

"Ex-sea captain. I asked you what you wanted!"

"I'm your nephew, Uncle Tooth, and I've come to
visit you."

"Don't want company!" replied Uncle Tooth. "Go away!" And he returned to his fishing as if the subject was closed.

Corduroy started to leave. But then he thought he would try one more time, so he said, "Is it true you have been all over the world?"

Uncle Tooth set down his fishing pole and grunted. "Aye, that I have, all over the world and then some!"

"It must have been wonderful," said Corduroy. "I would love to see what the rest of the world looks like."

"It looks like many things," said Uncle Tooth.

"Like poetry?"

"Some of it." By now, Uncle Tooth didn't seem nearly so grouchy. He winked and said, "By jingo! You're the most inquisitive person I've met in twelve years! Come up here where I can see you."

Corduroy scrambled up the wet rocks and found himself face to face with the old sea captain. He could tell just by looking into Uncle Tooth's eyes that he wasn't looney. There was wisdom in them, and experience, and maybe a little sorrow.

"Now what do you want to know about?" So Corduroy told him. They sat there and talked for a long time, until a chill wind came up and Corduroy began to shiver. "Here," said Uncle Tooth, "come over to my shack—it's not far—and I'll give you something to warm you up."

Uncle Tooth drew in his line, put away his tackle, and stuffed the fish he'd caught into a dilapidated basket with a lid to it. Then he led the way, over more

rocks and up a slight hill to a small yard with an iron
gate. Inside the yard, nestled against the cliffs, stood a
weather-beaten shack. Uncle Tooth had constructed it
himself out of driftwood and salvage. It was a squat,
dark dwelling, moldy from the dampness, and it leaned
a tinge to one side.

Not far off, almost hidden amongst the rocks, stood
a sailing ship. It looked very old, the masts were bare,
and sailcloth covered most of it.

"Is that your ship?" Corduroy asked.

"No," replied his uncle. "That's the ship that

brought me here. I had a real ship once, a beauty of a vessel! But that was long ago . . . gone . . . washed away."

Fishing an ancient key out of his pea coat, Uncle Tooth unlocked the door of his shack, and they went inside.

When Uncle Tooth lit one of the lanterns, Corduroy saw that the place was infested with rats! They were all over—on the table, on the walls, and running along the rafters. Some of them ran into their holes in the wainscotting, but others, more bold, poked busy faces out from wherever they were hiding.

Hastily, Uncle Tooth searched for something to throw at them, but the only thing he could find was an old boot. "You ugly wee beasts!" he cursed. "Where were you when I needed you?" He flung the boot up to the ceiling, where it missed hitting a rat and got stuck in a crevice of the beams.

Grunting, he went over to the stove to brew some cocoa for Corduroy and a hot toddy (he put cinnamon in it) for himself. "I'll get 'em yet, the vermin!" he said.

While Uncle Tooth was busy, Corduroy walked around the shack. On the walls were framed pictures of magnificent sailing ships, and hanging from the rafters were old anchors and fishnets. Against one wall was a cabinet containing teas from all over the world and a variety of old drinking mugs with boats and dragons carved into them. A stained oak table, a stool, and an armchair fashioned from a barrel stood in the center of the room, grouped around a potbellied stove with pipes that extended out of a hole in the roof. And in the farthest corner was a hammock-bed where Uncle Tooth slept.

"Uh . . . nice place," said Corduroy.

Uncle Tooth responded with a grunt. "I have been here for a long time," he said, bringing the mugs over and setting them on the table, "with the floorboards creaking, and the shutters knocking at the wind, and above me, the rats treading like trolls across the ceiling. . . . My life is filled with noises that disrupt my thinking. . . . Here, drink this. The hot will be good for you."

Eagerly, Corduroy reached for the mug of cocoa. The inside of the shack was almost as cold as the afternoon, and he was still shivering. Uncle Tooth stocked the stove with pieces of driftwood. It popped and sputtered but failed to warm the drafty shack.

Uncle Tooth took down his pipe, packed the cup with tobacco from an old tin, and brought out blankets.

One he put over Corduroy's knees, and one over his own. He sat in his armchair next to the stove, puffing rings of smoke ceilingward. For a long while, they sat facing one another, sipping their drinks, not speaking.

Then Uncle Tooth muttered, almost to himself, "I rode the seas till I could ride no more, and I'd ride 'em again if I could."

17

Uncle Tooth looked to be in very good health, and Corduroy couldn't understand why he had given up his career. But instead of asking, he said, "Were you always a sailor?"

Uncle Tooth removed his pipe, stared at it, returned it to his mouth, and chewed on the stem in a thoughtful way. "Guess I always had a bit of the sea in my blood, even before I actually set foot upon it . . . even when I was very young . . . all my life."

"Tell me what it was like," said Corduroy.

"It was so lovely it makes my eyes water to recall it."

He continued to burn quantities of tobacco as the afternoon did dark things outside. And from the smoke grew mists of memory.

How Uncle Tooth
Fooled the Sea Lizard

I have never had but one ambition, and that was to go to sea.

My family have always been tradespeople. My great-grandpa Growl founded the local Five and Dime when this town was even smaller than it is now. After he retired, my grandpa took over, and then my father. I was expected to follow in their footsteps, but I always knew that the merchant's life was not for me.

Great and wondrous sailing vessels dropped anchor off the coast, and sailors came ashore to sell their cargo. Everyone was excited about the exotic spices and fabric and china, but I was more concerned about the places they came from. So I decided to live my life as a sailor.

My family didn't approve, especially your Auntie Hick. She thought it was my duty to stay and help your mother and her run the shop after Father retired—but I have always been a determined alligator.

When I grew up, I packed my few belongings in a knapsack, took my savings, and prepared to go off to one of the large seaports where ships set sail to distant lands. The day I left, Hick told me, "You have absolutely no experience. Who will hire you? You're too adventurous for your own good! Just wait—you're going to end up with nothing!"

"And you're too practical!" I called as I started down

the street. "We'll see who ends up with nothing!"

In one respect she was right: since I had no experience at sailing, I would have to rely upon my wits to get a job. I traveled over mountains and through valleys, until I arrived at the seaport of Catfish Bay.

A yellow fog hung low over the town, engulfing the building tops and settling like a giant coverlet over the cobbled streets. Here and there, orange glows indicated windows or streetlamps.

I soon found my way to a narrow shop that sold, in addition to food and dry goods, all the things you would need at sea. With half my savings, I purchased a sailor's suit. It was white with red stripes. And a sailor's cap. It was woolly and was good for keeping your ears warm. Last of all, I got a spyglass to sight ships through. After putting on all my new clothes, I felt grand indeed!

"Ho!" said the shopkeeper. "Yer a fine sight! Where are you going all dressed up?"

"I'm going to become a sailor of the seas," said I.

The shopkeeper just shut one eye and looked at me in a puzzled way. "No ships have set sail from Catfish Bay these three weeks, nor many more come in," he said.

I couldn't get him to explain further, although he was kind enough to direct me to the local inn. After my long journey, I had need of some refreshment.

The inn was a cramped, noisy place full of sailors. In the heavy smoke they were nearly faceless, but I could hear the laughter, the clink of silver, and the ring of beer mugs knocking together.

Seating myself at an empty table in the corner, I ordered a bowl of carrot soup and thought about what the shopkeeper had said. In the next booth, some sailors were discussing their troubles.

"Blast the infernal monster!" cried a rough, grizzly voice. "As long as he stays, there will be no shipping trade from Catfish Bay!"

"But who's to get rid of him, tell me that?" someone else said.

"I've tried everything," the first voice went on. "Sharp harpoons, cannons, torpedoes . . . hah! The monster makes toothpicks out of them!"

Slipping out of my seat, I went over to the booth; and making my voice sound courageous, I said, "What's this about a monster?"

Seated round the table were three rather tough-looking characters: an orange cat, a sleek brown ferret, and a fat old bear. All wore nautical attire and all were drinking from large mugs of beer. The old bear was an imposing fellow. His fur, somewhat matted, smelled of brine, and he was one-eyed and lame to boot, but he was obviously the leader since he spoke up first.

"What? You mean you don't know?"

Before I could answer, the orange cat sniffed, "Must be a stranger!"

At this, I told them my history and my ambition to become a sailor. The ferret and the cat began snickering, but the old bear scowled and said, "Enough of that! I'll not have you laughing at anyone who loves the sea!"

The cat and ferret immediately got quiet.

"I'm Captain Paddler Poopdeck," the old bear went on. "And these are my cronies, Tugboat Tod and Little Quee. Squeeze in here beside us and I'll tell you about our problem."

Captain Poopdeck leaned forward, elbows on the table, and began in a deep, raspy voice:

24

CAPTAIN POOPDECK'S TALE

Aside from being a busy seaport, Catfish Bay is the site of a large mandarin orange cannery. Mandarin oranges are shipped here from various parts of the world to be peeled, packed in cans, and sent out to stores to be sold. So they bring in quite a lot of trade.

Three weeks ago—it was a wild and moonless night, I remember—a giant Sea Lizard appeared out of nowhere, came ashore, and broke into the cannery. After devouring every single mandarin orange in sight (rinds included), he slid over to the lighthouse on Lone Point, curled his ugly body round it, and took a snooze. Scared the poor lighthouse keeper half out of his wits! And the beast has been there ever since. Sometimes, on a foggy day such as this, he'll flash his fiery red eyes, and sea captains, thinking it is the lighthouse, sail right into his clutches. At other times, he creates a great wind with his breath and sucks in ships from as far off as thirty miles. Then he gobbles up their entire cargo, spits out what isn't edible, and swallows the rest. He'll eat almost anything; but oranges are his favorite food.

To make matters worse, a group of pirates under the leadership of Captain Hoot the Horrible have turned this to their advantage. Their galleon is anchored in a lagoon down the coast where the monster can't see them (he stays pretty close to Lone

Point). After the Sea Lizard has destroyed a ship and had a good meal, he goes to his bed on the ocean floor and takes a long nap. Then the pirates move in and gather up what's left of the cargo.

Oh, it's a terrible tragedy! Soon Catfish Bay will be ruined, for everybody will be afraid to come here. And I shall be ruined, too, unless I can put out to sea shortly.

Captain Poopdeck peered into his beer mug, as if the answer to his troubles lay at the bottom of the glass.

I had listened to his story with much interest, and a plan was beginning to form in my mind. "I'll do it," I said. "I'll take care of the Sea Lizard for you."

All three of them broke into fits of wild laughter. Pounding the table, Captain Poopdeck bellowed, "Ho! Ho! You make me laugh, you little nut!"

Tugboat Tod giggled and said, "Why, you look like a miniature sea lizard yourself!"

This set off a new round of laughter. I waited until they had finished, then added, "And I'll get rid of the pirates, too, while I'm at it."

My serious attitude had a sobering effect upon them, and Captain Poopdeck asked, "But how? How will you do it?"

"I haven't quite figured that out yet," I said. "It depends . . . *but*, if I do succeed in eliminating the Sea Lizard and the pirates, I shall expect a reward."

"You name it, I'll pay it," replied Captain Poopdeck.

"I'd like a job on your ship."

"Granted," said the Captain.

I rose to leave. "Well, good-bye for now. I have things to attend to, but I'll be in touch." And with that, I strutted out through the smoky room with much more confidence than I had when I'd entered.

The fog had lifted, and Catfish Bay was shining peacefully under a warm afternoon sun. It was hard to believe that the terrible Sea Lizard lurked so near. Getting rid of that monster and a crew of pirates would not be easy, but becoming a sailor was so important to me, I was willing to risk the danger. "Every problem has its solution," I thought as I headed toward the beach.

When I asked several passersby the way to Lone Point, they trembled and stared at me as if I was mad. Finally, one old fisherman pointed at a stretch of rolling dunes and said the lighthouse lay just beyond them.

I have the advantage of being small, so I was able to sneak up behind the dunes quietly, without arousing too much attention. When I felt I was close enough, I took out my new spyglass and fixed it on the lighthouse. It looked deserted. Then I slowly scanned the surrounding water. The Sea Lizard was nowhere in sight.

Deciding that he must be asleep somewhere, I left and climbed to the top of a group of cliffs on the other side of the point. I walked along them until I located the lagoon where the pirate galleon was anchored.

I flattened myself on the warm rocks and peered through my spyglass. The pirates' ship was a round,

dark frigate manned by rows of shiny cannons, with crimson sails; and flying from its mast was that dreaded flag—the skull and crossbones! I could see many rough and dirty-looking pirates lounging on the deck, eating, playing games, or singing songs. A nasty lot!

Next, I surveyed the lagoon itself: the rocks, the water, and the entrance from the sea. When I had seen everything I wanted, I headed back to Catfish Bay.

Captain Poopdeck, Tugboat Tod, and Little Quee were seated on stools in front of the General Store wearing long expressions.

"How do!" I called, strutting up.

Captain Poopdeck removed the corncob pipe he had been smoking and said, "Caught that Sea Lizard yet?"

"No," I answered, "but I have a plan that I think will

work. What I need from you is a small boat, with just
enough room for me, my knapsack, and maybe a
bucket of paint."

"That can be easily arranged," Captain Poopdeck
said.

Offering no further explanation, I went into the General Store and purchased a bucket of orange paint and
a wide paintbrush.

That night, Captain Poopdeck took me down to the
stone seawall at the edge of the pier where a little boat
was tied.

"This is my private rowboat," the Captain informed me. "Since it is painted blue, it ought to be good camouflage in the dark. . . . Are you sure you know what you're doing?"

"Don't worry," I said as I climbed in. "I'll return your boat safe and sound in the morning." Then I cast off into the dark and dangerous ocean. My little boat moved like a dart through the great motion of the sea, and soon I lost sight of Captain Poopdeck's lantern.

The sky became filled with little lights and a curl of moon, and I was able to tell where I was. Silently as possible, I paddled toward the pirates' lagoon. It seemed like forever before I reached the entrance. As I drifted in, I saw the lights from the pirates' galleon dancing on the water and heard the sounds of merriment. Evidently the pirates were having a party.

Tying my boat to a rock, I took the can of paint in one paw, held the brush between my teeth, and dove into the icy water. I am an excellent swimmer, and in no time at all, I found myself abreast with the tall, black hull of the galleon. I swam about until I spotted an open porthole, grabbed on to the planks with my free paw, and hoisted myself out of the water. Cautiously I peeked inside. Luck was with me; I was below deck, looking into a storeroom.

I crawled through the porthole and dropped to the floor. The room was filled almost to the brim with stolen loot: everything from jewels and crowns to fancy clothes and elegant furniture. I stood motionless for a moment, awed by it all. Then I realized that this was

not the room I wanted. So I tiptoed to the door.

Outside was a narrow hallway lit by a lantern, and in a chair leaning against the wall, a greasy, bearded pirate was snoring loudly.

Swallowing hard, I very carefully slid out the door, entered a room directly opposite, and breathed a sigh of relief. This was the one I had been seeking—the weapon room! Inside were pistols, knives, swords, extra cannons, and most important to me, a large pile of cannon balls.

Now the real work began. I pried the lid off the orange paint can, dipped in my brush, and began to paint every single cannon ball. It was exhausting work and took me the entire night, but I kept at it until all the cannon balls looked like fresh, juicy oranges.

Long before I finished, I heard snoring above me; the pirates had drunk themselves into a stupor.

Just as a pinkish dawn hovered over the horizon, I slid out of a porthole and swam back to my waiting boat. The first part of my plan was complete.

The ocean was at peace, as all things are in the very early morning, and there was still no sign of the Sea Lizard.

When I got within sight of the lighthouse, I stopped rowing, opened my knapsack, and drew out a mandarin orange that I happened to have brought from home. I sat down and slowly started to peel it, tossing the rinds overboard.

All of a sudden, there was a churning in the water. Bubbles rose to the surface and popped. The sea became frothy and swirled in eerie patterns. With a sudden rush and a gigantic shower, the Sea Lizard emerged from the ocean depths. He towered above my little boat, as tall as nine masts, all green and scaly, with a head that looked like a watermelon.

He stretched his shiny coils, wiggled his ugly snout from side to side, and glared at me with his awful red eyes.

"I SMELL MANDARIN ORANGES!" he roared. "AND JUST IN TIME FOR BREAKFAST!"

I was frightened, but I answered, "Only one . . . *one* mandarin orange, and it's *my* breakfast." And I continued to slowly peel the mandarin orange.

This confused the Lizard for a second. He wasn't

used to folks answering him back. But he opened his huge jaws and chuckled. "NOT SO! NOT SO! IF YOU DON'T GIVE IT TO ME AT ONCE, I'LL TURN YOU AND YOUR BOAT INTO DRIFT-WOOD!" The monster darted his tongue along his lips as if he could taste the orange already.

Heaving a sigh, I said, "Oh, very well. If you insist upon being a bully about it." Acting very reluctant to part with my orange, I gave it one last look, then threw it straight at the monster. He leaned forward, snapped it up in midair, and swallowed it whole.

It pleased me that he didn't bother to chew his food, because it meant my plan had an even better chance of succeeding.

"ANY MORE?" inquired the monster hopefully.

"There's a whole cargo of ripe oranges right under your very nose, just waiting to be eaten," I answered. "But you'll never find them."

"WHERE?" cried the monster.

"While you've been sleeping under the sea, a gang of clever pirates have stolen all the choicest oranges and kept them for themselves."

The Sea Lizard's awful eyes glowed like fire; he clamped his claws together and gnashed his teeth. "OH, SO!" he hissed. "TELL ME WHERE THESE PIRATES ARE, OR I'LL BITE YOUR LITTLE HEAD OFF!"

"You are a terribly rude person," I replied. "But I guess I have no choice. The pirates' galleon is anchored in a lagoon behind those rocks over there, and the hold is full of the largest oranges you've ever seen. Maybe if you ask politely, they'll give you some."

And I began laughing as if I thought the monster wasn't the least bit frightening. I knew it would make him crazy with anger.

Hissing and spewing smoke, the Sea Lizard sped off through the water toward the lagoon.

I rowed to shore and climbed up the cliffs, hoping to get a good view of what would happen next. There wasn't time to get very close, but my spyglass helped.

I could see all of Captain Hoot's men running about. Then, with one swift flick of his claw, the monster knocked an immense hole in the deck. A joyful grin spread across his face, and I knew he had found the cannon balls. Bending down, he began to gobble them whole. It wasn't until he'd swallowed the very last one that he realized they weren't oranges. With a thunderous groan, he lost his balance, toppled across the pirates' galleon, then quickly sank out of sight, dragging it with him.

Most of the pirates had abandoned ship in time. Some were swimming to shore, while others were putting out to sea in rowboats. With their galleon and all their ammunition gone, I knew nobody would have to worry about them for a while.

I hurried down the cliffs to wake the townspeople and let them know that they would be troubled by the Sea Lizard and the pirates no longer.

When Captain Poopdeck first heard my story, he was too amazed to speak. Then he broke into a jubilant laugh and said, "I must confess, I didn't think you could do it. You're small, but you have brains, and you'll need them if you're going to work for me. Welcome to my crew."

And that's how I became a sailor of the seas!

How Uncle Tooth
Went Looking for Fame

Corduroy began to spend most of his time visiting with Uncle Tooth, listening to his tales of adventure. They discovered that they both had curious natures and both were facinated by the sea. "You remind me of me when I was young," Uncle Tooth often said.

Of course, Auntie Hick didn't know where Corduroy was spending his free time these days, and he never told her for fear of her nerves. It was his secret.

One day when Corduroy arrived at the shack, Uncle Tooth handed him a thin parcel wrapped in dirty canvas. "Here," he said. "This is for you. A present from your old uncle."

Excitedly, Corduroy unwound the canvas to find a

shiny copper spyglass. On the handle was a gold plate that said TOOTH. "Oh, Uncle Tooth, it's lovely! But don't you want it anymore?"

"What for?" laughed his uncle. "I don't need that to see the rats! Come on outside."

They went to the edge of the highest cliff. Looking through the spyglass, Corduroy could see birds which were hundreds of feet up, ships far off on the horizon, and a pale moon rising in a still light sky. "The moon is up early today!" he cried. "And look! There the sun is sinking. I wonder where it goes."

Uncle Tooth laughed again. "You know, I wondered about that too, once, and a voyage grew out of my curiosity. It is a tale about searching."

For years I sailed on Captain Poopdeck's ship, and my life was one exciting adventure after another. I had many friends and made a good salary, but I soon began to feel like just one of a number. I wanted to do something special that would make me unique.

At dusk of every day, I'd see the narrow fishing boats easing into port, black against the last brilliant show of sun. The sails floated on their masts like kites, tinged with an edge of gold. Then, wild and red, the sun slipped quietly beyond the water at a place where the ocean met the sky.

I wanted to be there when the sun disappeared, to see where it went at night. Did it go down beneath the waves and light the ocean floor, or did it turn all flat and lose its glow? And why did it come up again on the other side of the sky? But no matter how far I traveled on Captain Poopdeck's ship, that place was always a long way off. So I asked my mates, Dirty Mo the Barge Bear and Tugboat Tod and Little Quee, but none of them had been there either.

Then I thought if I could be the first to discover that place where the ocean meets the sky, I would be famous. All the sailors would look up to me, and someone might even write a song about my adventure. So I said good-bye to my mates, took leave of Captain Poopdeck, and prepared to set forth on my quest.

First, I went to work constructing a stout, strong boat, for it would be a long journey. For many days I labored on the boat until it had everything I needed: a mast with a sail, coils of rope, a searchlight, and a cabin. Inside the cabin was a steering wheel that faced two windows. Out of these windows I could see everything ahead of me, but there was a curtain that could be drawn across in case I wanted privacy. In the back, a cozy bed was set against the wall next to a porthole, so that at night I could look out at the stars. In the far corner stood a coal-burning stove with a shelf beside it stocked with food. Lining the walls near the front of the cabin were pictures of my three closest friends, Dirty Mo, Tugboat Tod, and Little Quee.

Next, I laid in a large store of provisions: tea and whole-wheat biscuits, avocadoes, cheese, and soybeans. I brought an accordian to sing to and a book with lined pages to write down all I saw.

One gray morning, when almost everyone was asleep, I had my last bowl of carrot soup at the inn. Within an hour I was well at sea, the sharp air pulling my little boat through the waves, bound for unknown waters. There's nothing more pleasant than to be headed in a direction where new experiences and ad-

venture can be found. Getting out my accordian, I sang:

> With a yo ho hee
> I'll sail the sea,
> And a happier chap
> There never will be!

For two weeks nothing happened. The ocean was a silent companion, and every time I passed by a harbor with other ships, it made me lonesome for my friends. I recalled how we used to meet all those winter evenings in port between voyages, under the warm lanterns of the public houses where we sang and drank

and told grand tales of our exploits on the high seas.
Ah, the camaraderie!

Suddenly the wind wailed, the waters churned, and
huge drops of rain shot down from the clouds. My little
boat got tossed about like a barrel. I ran inside the
cabin, bolted the door, and peeked through a porthole.
How rapidly the black clouds hurtled through the air!
I could hear the thunder, low and solemn, far away yet
drawing nearer. Then the sky was alive with white
flashes—lightning! My boat skimmed along on the
crest of the waves. The sails tore, and some of the
provisions got swept overboard.

Eventually the storm passed. Poking my head cautiously out of the cabin, I saw that the storm had washed a whole mess of dead fish onto the deck—only that was no help to me, for I'm a vegetarian.

There was nothing to do but drift. When the sky cleared, a welcome sun peeked through, and I breathed in the crisp, clean air that the rain always brings. I got out my spyglass to see if there was land nearby.

There was just a long line of barren terrain with dry grass blowing in the breeze, and in the water, dozens of oddly shaped rocks. Some of the rocks looked almost like houses, with windows carved into their surfaces. Then I noticed a ragged gray rock, larger than the others, which seemed to be a fortress of some kind. Numerous brown pelicans were perched upon it in sentinel fashion. Some of them were gazing out to sea, while others marched back and forth as if they were guarding something. Down at the bottom of the rock was a window with stone bars across it, and inside stood a little puffin bird looking sad as a lost ship.

I remembered hearing about the feud which the pelicans and puffins had been carrying on for years. The pelicans said it was their water, and they were entitled to all the fish; the puffins insisted no, the water belonged to them, and they owned whatever they caught. It seemed silly to me, all this fighting over something that can't really belong to anybody. But, to be honest, I was on the side of the puffins, since they are little birds and no match for the arrogant pelicans.

I thought and thought how I might get that little

puffin out of his prison cell. I knew I couldn't reason with the pelicans; I'd have to use my wits. Then I had an idea.

I quickly moved all the fish the storm had washed onto the deck into my rowboat. Then I climbed in myself and lowered it into the water. I had to do it very carefully so the pelicans wouldn't hear me. I rowed over to a flat rock some ways off. Depositing the fish on the rock, I turned round and came by the other side where the pelicans could see me. They looked stern and bobbed their great bills, but said not a word.

"Ahoy!" I cried, trying to sound excited. "A mess of puffins are having a feast on that rock over yonder. They said they are tired of taking sass from you pelicans and from now on they intend to eat as much fish as they please!"

The pelicans began jabbering amongst themselves. Then—by jingo!—they all flew off at once. As soon as they were out of sight, I drew my rowboat closer and jumped out onto the steps of the fortress. The prison door was blocked by a large stone, but I managed to roll it aside—and out popped the puffin.

He was so happy to be free, he started to do a hornpipe (that is a sailor's dance). "Quick!" I cried. "Get into the boat!"

Hopping in, I grabbed the oars, and when the puffin followed, I began rowing away as fast as I could. The puffin kept looking over his shoulder anxiously.

"Don't worry, mate," said I. "The pelicans will be occupied with the fish for a good bit." Then to my

horror, I remembered that my ship was without a sail and couldn't go anyplace at all. I tried to explain to the puffin. He looked startled, then quickly flew out of the boat.

"There's gratitude!" I cried.

The puffin didn't fly off, however; he circled above me. And each time he made a circle, he rose higher and higher until he was just a dark dot in the air. "Queer as the tides," I thought.

At last the puffin seemed to stop, and when he returned, he was dragging, in his beak, a small white cloud—a perfect sail!

By now, I had reached my ship. With the puffin's help, I removed the torn sail and fastened the cloud to the mast, where it looked like a transparent sheet. A gust of wind came along just then and pushed the sail which moved the ship, and we sped out to sea. "You're a clever old bird," said I to the puffin. "And I need a friend to keep me company. How would you like to be my first mate?"

The puffin fluffed his wings, stuck out his chest, and squawked. "That's mighty kind of you," he replied. "I, too, could use a friend. You may think that it's just the pelicans who cause trouble. Not so. We puffins have quick tempers and are always fighting among ourselves. In fact, that's how I wound up in prison. Me and another puffin got into a dispute over some fish we had caught. He thought the fish ought to be divided evenly, but I thought I should get most of them since I had done the most work. Well, pretty soon our squawking

turned to biting and clawing. We were atop a tall rock.
and finally tumbled off and plunged into the sea,
locked together in combat. When we hit the water, I
lost consciousness. Some pelicans must have come
along then, because when I came to, there I was in
prison! I tell you, it will be a relief to get away from all
this squabbling."

"Well, if you stay with me," I replied, "I promise I'll
always respect your efforts and see that you get credit
for them."

The puffin looked extremely grateful. "Then it's a
sailor's life for me," he said.

And so he stayed. I taught the puffin the rudiments
of nautical life: how to knot ropes, use a compass, read
maps, and work a steering wheel. And in between les-
sons, I told him about my life, my friends, and my
quest. The puffin listened seriously, but every now and

then he'd shake his head. "To think you had all those friends and you left them. . . . It must be easy to give up something you have a lot of."

"No," I answered. "It's not easy. But I don't feel important enough. I have to do something no one else has ever done."

The puffin shook his head again and peered out to sea.

For many days we sailed through temperate waters, past sunny green isles, enjoying our work and each other's company. At night the puffin stood on the prow of the ship, holding a lantern in his beak to light our way. I remained in the cabin studying maps and charting our course.

One day I told the puffin, "Tomorrow, according to my calculations, we'll pass the last stretch of land, and then there will be nothing ahead but the open sea."

"How lonely it sounds," he said quietly.

"There's only one problem," I said. "You can always catch fish to eat, but most of my provisions were washed overboard in the storm. I'm down to my last biscuit. I should stock up on food, but alas, I have no more money." And heaving a sigh, I thought about the delicious, thick carrot soup I used to eat at the inn.

The puffin cocked his head and shut one eye. "You're right," he said. "Food has always been available to me, so I've never had any need for money. . . . Tell me, what phase will the moon be in tonight?"

"Full, I believe."

"Ah!" cried the puffin. "We're in luck then! Just

watch with me tonight, and I think your problem will
be solved."

I removed my cap and scratched my head in confu-
sion. Sometimes the puffin seemed to talk in riddles.

But that night I sat with him and watched the round
moon slowly slide into an inky sky.

Dousing the lantern, the puffin whispered, "We must
have maximum darkness. I've observed this many
times. Now, keep your eye on that section of water
over there."

As the moon rose higher, its brightness increased
until its reflection made the water shimmer like jewels.

We sat silently, watching the lights dancing on the waves. By jingo! They *were* jewels!

Fetching a net, the puffin and I flung it into the ocean just where the moon's reflection was, and when we pulled the net in, some of the moon's jewels had clung to it. All night we fished for jewels on the quiet sea. By morning, we had caught twenty-four of them, which I placed in my purse. "We're rich!" I cried. "What a valuable old bird you are!"

"Squawk!" said the puffin.

It was a good omen, though we still didn't have any food, and my confidence returned once more. As the sun of a new day stretched its way over the water, I took my accordian and sang:

> *With a yo ho hum*
> *And the moon and the sun*
> *And a cloud on the mast*
> *Of a ship on the sea,*
> *There isn't a happier chap than me!*

At midday a brisk wind moved the ship toward a green coast, the last bit of land before the open sea. Salt-white cottages sparkled in the sun on hills above a bay. The only building on the beach was a house that had been fashioned from an upturned boat, and before the house sat a fat, leathery old woman surrounded by baskets and barrels of fish.

I dropped anchor and went ashore, the puffin following after me. "Ahoy!" I called. "I am Captain Tooth of that rig yonder, and this is my first mate."

"How do," said the old woman. "I'm Penelope Freshfish. Looking to buy some seafood?"

I explained I was a vegetarian, but that I would buy some for the puffin. All at once, a marvelous fragrance wafted from the houseboat and tickled my nose. It smelled exactly like carrot soup! "Do you sell carrot soup as well?" I asked eagerly.

Penelope Freshfish gave a silent, amused laugh and rocked back and forth like a wave. "No, that I don't. But if you would care to join me for lunch, I'll *give* you some," she said.

Well, I did not need to be asked twice. We followed

the old woman into her dark house. It looked like a
shipwreck! Penelope cleared some sewing from the
table, then got down bowls and mugs and cheese and
croutons, and brewed tea. It was a wonderful meal—
and oh, that carrot soup! It was a happier discovery
than any treasure.

For a long while, everybody was too busy eating to
talk. Then Penelope said, "Where are you headed all by
yourselves?"

"On a great quest," I said. "We've been traveling for
many days and nights, over many miles. We're going

to discover the place where the ocean meets the sky. Then we'll be famous, and maybe rich, too. Yo hee!"

The old woman just smiled, not jolly like before, but wistfully, as if she was recalling something very precious. Then she told us this story:

PENELOPE'S TALE

When I was a young lass, I dreamed of being a fine lady, of having a grand house and lovely clothes and expensive jewels. Then I met the fishmonger. He wasn't fancy, but he had a good heart, and he promised that someday he'd give me all the things I wanted.

So we got married and moved to this little houseboat. It's just temporary, he says. And every day I'd watch him go out to sea in his little boat to catch fish. And while he was away, I would dream about having the grand house and the jewels and all —just like that fisherman's wife in the fairy tale. But in the evening when I'd see his boat coming in, my dreaming seemed foolish because I knew the fishmonger would never be able to afford those things.

But he never stopped promising them to me. For thirty years he treated me like a fine lady, and now he is dead. I never did get my grand house or my lovely clothes or my expensive jewels. But, you know, I think if I had them, I'd give them all up just to see his little boat coming in once more.

There are dreams, the kind you feel when you sleep, and dreams of something good you hope will come in the future; but most lasting are the dreams you have of someone you loved and will never see again.

When Penelope had finished her story, she brushed a tear from her eye and said she was only a silly old woman. For several minutes, I simply sat there, not saying a word; then I rose and whispered something to the puffin. He nodded, so I opened my purse and emptied the moon-jewels onto the table. They illuminated the dark houseboat and made Penelope's eyes sparkle. She gave a gasp of delight.

"Here," I told her. "These are for you. They are payment for the soup, and also for the very great favor you have done me. What a silly alligator I am! Leaving all my dear friends for something I might never find, or something I wouldn't know what to do with once I'd found it. I think it's time I went back home."

Penelope patted my paw. She gave us some saltine crackers, a hunk of cheese, and a full pot of carrot soup. So I left her there in her little houseboat by the sea, and the puffin and I turned the boat round the way we had come.

"You know," I told him as we headed back to Catfish Bay, "I just realized that having a purpose in life is not doing something great, but doing something well—and enjoying what you're doing. I didn't find the place where the ocean meets the sky—though I suppose I'll

never stop dreaming about it—but I found out what I
really want to do. I'm going back to my mates!"

"Hooray!" shouted the puffin.

And taking my accordian, I sang:

> With a yo ho hoo
> And a very fine crew
> And work and songs
> On the rollicking sea,
> There isn't a happier chap than me!

So I returned home and went back to work for Captain Poopdeck, and the puffin signed on as the ship's
scout. As I think back on it now, those were the best
years of my life—working the sea with all my friends
—the very best!

How Uncle Tooth
Lost Everything

One fall day, Corduroy went with his Uncle Tooth down the pier to the Dry Goods Shop. It stood apart from the rest of the town: an old, weathered building, gray as rain clouds.

Inside it was just as dark and dreary, but there were many curious things on the counters for Corduroy to examine. Uncle Tooth purchased oil for his lanterns, soap, tobacco, matches, rum for his hot toddies—and, of course, some traps! He had bought, at one time or another, every available rat poison on the market, as well as cages, boxes, and snares.

The Dry Goods Man was used to Uncle Tooth, so he made sure there was always a supply of rat traps on

hand. As Uncle Tooth paid for his purchases, the Dry
Goods Man said, "By now, I imagine you would have
caught every rat who ever squeaked."

"No, by jingo!" replied Uncle Tooth. "There are always more of the horrid critters! Vicious vermin! A
plague upon rodents for the plague they are to me!"
With these ominous words, Uncle Tooth stalked out of
the shop with Corduroy close behind him.

It was a bright, wild, windy day, and the weather
seemed to be enjoying itself. Breakers dashed against
the rocks below with triumphant shouts, as Corduroy

and Uncle Tooth threaded their way along the cliffs. As soon as they were inside the shack, Corduroy said, "Why do you hate rats so much?"

"Why?" cried Uncle Tooth. "I'll tell you why: rats are the reason I retired from the sea (the spiteful devils!)."

"But you put up with all that other stuff: sea lizards, and pirates, and typhoons. How could some little rats end your career?"

"How indeed!" said Uncle Tooth. "It's a queer tale and a sad one."

In my years as a sailor, I made acquaintance with all the seven seas, journeyed to distant lands of wealth and mystery, saw strange and marvelous sights that most people only dream about, and made friends in every port of call from here to the Northern Isles. Finally, I even became captain of my own ship. The *Lizzie Mae* I called her, after a dance hall performer I'd seen and admired in my youth.

Ah, she was a wonder of a ship, three-masted and long as a whale! And many a fine voyage we made on her, hunting for tuna and lobsters, or shipping cargo to fair cities.

I had a crew of nine—some of them old friends,

others new—and I worked them hard, darned if I didn't! They slept in berths below deck, beneath my cabin and above the hold. The hold was where the rats lived.

Now, I never did care for rats, but every ship has them. And besides, they kept to themselves down there in the hold. Occasionally, one would pop on deck to chew a bit of rope and watch the high waves parting in the path of the ship; but I think they were fearful of the gulls, for we didn't see much of them.

There came a time when I had been everywhere, seen everything, done most of it, and now I was bored. For three months, the *Lizzie Mae* sat empty in the harbor while I pondered what to do next. My friends Dirty Mo and Little Quee were semi-retired, only making short, easy voyages when they felt like it. And Tugboat Tod had been lost at sea, presumably killed in a pirate raid. Although this was discouraging, I was determined not to retire, not old Tooth!

One day as I was lounging on the pier, smoking and gazing out over the horizon, who should happen by but the puffin. I hadn't seen him for many months, for he, too, was no longer a sailor. He had saved his pennies and had opened an amusement park a ways down the coast. But every now and then, we would get together to discuss old times.

"They tell me you're at a loss," he said right off. "I'm disgusted with you! A sailor's place is on the sea, not dilly-dallying about wharfs and messing round in boat shops."

"I'm bored," I said. "There is no adventure left. I've done it all, yet I'm still young enough to want more."

"You need a quest," said the puffin.

"That I do," said I.

Settling himself upon a post, the puffin cocked his head and gave me a reproving look. He waited until he collected his thoughts before he spoke. "Now, when I met you, you were on a quest—to discover where the sun sets, I believe. Whether or not you ever found it makes no difference; you had a goal, and that kept you excited. Now then, take a glance at this bit of parchment I came across recently."

Reaching inside his Windbreaker, the puffin produced a piece of cracked, yellow foolscap which he very carefully handed to me. Unrolling it, I found it to be a crudely drawn map of some kind, quite old. On the upper left corner were written these words:

> *Where the white whale whistles,*
> *Where the sea lions sing*
> *And six young sea horses dance in a ring,*
> *Below a moon, beneath a cove,*
> *A rich notorious treasure trove.*

At the bottom was a signature and a date. I could barely make out the scrawl, but it looked like C. HOOT.

"Why, do you know what this is?" I cried. "This must be a map of the lost hoard of Captain Hoot, the pirate. Where in heaven did you get it?"

"One of the children brought it to me. She discovered it rolled in a corked bottle stuck in the sand of one of those caves down the coast."

Jumping to my feet, I waved the parchment in the air. "Why, this is terrific! Yo hee! Fate has sent this so that I may have a new adventure."

"Fate and a little help from me," replied the puffin.

I lost no time. The very next day, I had a notice printed and distributed round the docks, which read:

THE *LIZZIE MAE* (CAPTAIN TOOTH, OWNER)
TO SET SAIL FROM CATFISH BAY AUGUST 8
ON IMPORTANT BUSINESS.
GOOD WAGES AND OPPORTUNITY FOR
ADVENTURE. SIGN NOW.

Well, scores of sailors turned up at the shipping office to apply for positions on my ship. They were all eager to join until they learned my destination. You see, the map indicated that the treasure was located somewhere beyond the Bubble Reefs in the Sea of Spume, a dark, uncharted, dangerous place of terrible legend. Stories of ships lost there had been circulating for years. Some claimed the stories to be true; others said that it was just superstitious nonsense. But all were too scared to find out for themselves. The Sea of Spume was one place I had never been, but legends didn't frighten me.

So I tried to talk the sailors into going, but no luck; not a one would sign. And the *Lizzie Mae* remained empty in the harbor.

I was so discouraged, I went to the inn for a bowl of carrot soup, and the puffin joined me. "Sailors were brave when I was a lad," I said, "but now they are afraid of their own shadows. I wish Dirty Mo or Little Quee were here, not that they would go anyway. What about you, Puffin?"

The puffin, who preferred slurping his soup while it was hot, instead of blowing on it, eyed me suspiciously. "Come now, Captain, I've got my amusement park to look after. Besides, I ain't as young as I was. The wings get rusty, you know. No . . . no . . . things are cozy here. What do I want to go adventuring for at my age? I've earned my comfort."

I snorted. "Ain't there nobody with any spirit left?"

Just then, we noticed at a table to our right an obese and rather decrepit-looking rat trading sass with the

innkeeper. "Mind how you treat your betters!" he cried in a shrill little voice. "I've been more places than you can guess. Give me the chance and I'd go again. Can't keep me in one spot for long. Another beer, matey!"

The innkeeper frowned, but he knew the rat had money to spend, so he brought the beer. The old rat gave a hearty squeak and pounded his mug upon the table. "Yo ho ho, ya swabs!" He laughed. "Pieces of eight . . . pieces of eight!" Then he took out a pocket-handkerchief and blew his nose.

Suddenly, I had a wild idea. I thought, "What if I staffed my ship with sailor rats? The rats were always on board, like it or not; why not make use of them?"

63

Approaching the old rat, I inquired if he was interested in leading a crew of his fellows on a voyage of great importance.

"The sea's me mother and mate," he said. "And money buys more beer. Aye, I'll do it if the pay is tidy."

I assured him it would be. So the old rat took charge of collecting a good body of experienced rats, while I took charge of the rest of the preparations, and we were set. The puffin admitted to being skeptical. "Rodents can't be trusted," he stated. But nothing could stop me now.

On a fine warm day in August, the *Lizzie Mae* set sail with her crew of sailor rats, in search of Captain Hoot's lost treasure.

After we had been at sea for only a few days, the puffin's warning began to make sense. Bustling about in a nervous way, the rats appeared to be busy. But when I paid attention, I saw that they did more bustling than work. They crawled everywhere, except up the mast to the crow's nest, where gulls might spot them. Indeed, every time the shadow of a bird slid over the ship, all the rats panicked and went to hide in the hold, where they spent their time eating up most of the provisions. You can imagine how disturbing this was. My only hope was that they would improve in time.

What a false hope that was! For the rats' true nature became evident the day we came to the Bubble Reefs! A thick border of large bubbly foam obscured the treacherous reefs that lay beyond. Using all my experience as a navigator, I guided the ship past the bubbles,

but then a northerly wind came up. The bubbles flew in the air and bounced off the sails. The *Lizzie Mae* rocked crazily to and fro.

The rats grew frightened and sent up a terrible squeaking. "Abandon ship!" I heard one of them scream.

I screamed back at them to stay where they were. The ship was leaning so far to one side that I feared she would plunge onto a reef at any moment; but in their panic, the rats all ran to the opposite side, and the weight caused the *Lizzie Mae* to right herself and tumble forward. Now she moved into open water, leaving the reefs behind. That was close. No wonder ships had a difficult time getting through.

I immediately called all the rats on deck and gave them a severe scolding. They promised not to panic next time, but I was beginning to distrust them.

Sending them back to their stations, I remained at the helm as the ship moved into the Sea of Spume. It was a singular place, green and flat as a piece of glass and so strangely silent that even the waves made whispers. But from far across the water came a sound—the high, hollow whistle of a great white whale. "Where the white whale whistles . . ." It was the first part of the riddle and meant the treasure must be close by.

At dusk, I sighted the whale himself, blowing a silver spray of water above his head. To the south was a thin stretch of rocky land that wound about in the shape of a snake. And at one end some strange animals, half cat, half fish, frolicked, making sharp, barking noises. "Where the sea lions sing . . ."

At this point, I thought it best to go the rest of the way alone in a rowboat. Dropping anchor, I called the old rat before me and gave him instructions for the maintenance of the ship in my absence. Then, taking a shovel and several sacks (to put the treasure in), I proceeded on my own.

As I drew closer to the rocks, some of the sea lions paused for an instant to observe me. "Ark! Ark!" they called. "Arooo!"

I slid past them cautiously, wondering where the dancing sea horses were. But then I came into the most enchanting little cove I had ever seen. It was surrounded by pointed rocks covered with lush vegetation, and at one end was a cave. "Below a moon, beneath a cove . . ."

By now, the moon was indeed lighting the bay. Things were almost frighteningly quiet. Suddenly, a small, echoish voice cried, "What kind of fish are you?"

Turning my head, I saw a delicate creature with tangled seaweed hair reclining on a rock. She had a catlike face, similar to the sea lions but more human. Her slim body was adorned with starfish and ocean vines, and it

tapered to a wide fishtail. She was a mermaid! "Can't you talk?" she said when I didn't answer.

"I'm not any kind of fish," I said. "I'm an alligator."

The mermaid paused for a moment, then repeated *alligator* to herself, quite slowly, as if she were saying it for the first time. "I have never seen an alligator before."

"Actually, I'm a sailor by trade; that's how I came here. Who are you?"

"My name is Silkie," she said, "and this is my cove. Isn't it lovely? On some nights the moon sparkles off the rocks, making them look almost transparent, like glass. Have you ever seen glass? I found a piece once, on the bottom of the sea. I guess it came from one of those moving rocks with the great white fins."

"Oh, you mean *ships*," I said.

"Is that what you call them? Once every season or so, a few will come by, but they never get close, and some of them sink. Is that a ship you are swimming in?"

"Not exactly—it's a rowboat, a smaller version."

Then I asked the mermaid if she knew of any sunken ships in the area, especially ones beneath the cove. But she shook her head right away.

"Oh, no. Ships never come to this little cove, not since I have been here. They would spoil its beauty." With that, she slid off the rock, dove into the water, and disappeared. But she was up again in no time, raising her head above the surface. "Once, years ago, when I was just a mer-child, an ugly looking fish who walked on his tail—he had *two* of them—came and placed a box of colored lights in my cave. Then he went away and I never saw him again. . . . But no ships have come."

"The colored lights," I cried excitedly. "What happened to them?"

The mermaid did a couple of backstrokes, then bobbed up and tossed her tangled hair. "Oh, they are still in my cave; most of them, that is. A few I gave to the sea lions to play with. Only the colored lights are no good since the colors get in the way. Real glass is clear, like water. Why do you ask?"

"Well, the truth is, I have made a special voyage in search of these colored lights, and they are very valuable to me."

"But you can't look *through* them. What good can they be?"

"May I see them anyway?" I asked.

The mermaid laughed and told me to follow her. Then she dove into the water and swam toward her cave. I paddled behind her. When I reached the mouth of the cave, I moored the boat and entered on foot. Directly inside was a short, narrow tunnel with walls that were moist with fungus. The cave was dimly lit, but I could see the mermaid's blue tail flicking back and forth in front of me.

Soon we came to an oval-shaped room that had a fishy smell to it. Luminous light from a hole in the ceiling bounced off the green walls. In one corner was a shelf that held the mermaid's possessions: a bone comb, some shells, and a tiny mirror. Below this was

her bed, set on a flat stone. And at the foot of the bed, a group of sea horses were dancing on their tails, round an ancient, rusty chest. The chest was open, and I saw that it was filled to the brim with thousands of rubies, emeralds, and diamonds.

"There they are," said the mermaid. "Sometimes the

light keeps me awake, but by now I'm almost used to it."

No wonder she called them colored lights, for they sparkled like stars. "Why don't you close the lid?" I said, but then noticed that it was rusted in place.

The mermaid frowned as if she had just thought of something. "If you could help me take the colored lights away, maybe that box would make a good bed. I've thought of that before, only who wants to sleep on a lot of little stones? But if it were empty . . ."

"You mean, you will give me the colored lights?" I cried.

"If they are that important to you," said the mermaid.

So I spent the whole night collecting the treasure. It was a slow job. First, I had to edge my way to the chest and load as many jewels as I could carry into the sacks. These I brought to the rowboat. And when it was full, I paddled out to the *Lizzie Mae* and stored the sacks in my cabin.

The rats were getting impatient and complained of a shortage of food, but I told them to sit tight, as we would be sailing for home in a few hours.

When I returned to the cove, the sun had come up. In the morning light, the mermaid had lost none of her strange beauty. When she climbed on a rock and the winds warmed her and the sun softly dried her, she still looked wet and wiggly, like a fish in a net, a small, sleek thing of the sea. She would toss her green hair, blink her coral eyes, remain perfectly stiff for as long as she

71

chose; then in a flash, she would slip back into the water to become once again a movement on the waves.

She swam alongside the rowboat, asking hundreds of questions about life beyond the Bubble Reefs. And the more questions she asked, the more magical she seemed. How opposite we were. While I had traveled all over the wide world, she had spent her entire life here in this lonely cove. I imagined showing her the places I had been and teaching her the things I knew. How unique it would be to have a mermaid with me always. Everyone would envy me. And on cold nights, when I was tired from sailing, what a comfort she would be to come home to!

I said, "Silkie, suppose I took you back to the mainland with me. Would you be happy?"

"I'm always happy. Please, may we go at once?"

I was surprised how quickly she agreed. I left her alone for a few minutes to say farewell to her cove. Then she came bouncing through the foam, slipped into the rowboat, and said, "Let's go!" I wrapped her in a blanket so she wouldn't catch cold, and we set off.

As I rowed out of the cove, I noticed all the sea lions were lined up on their rocks. They looked angry and began howling in unison, almost like a song.

"What on earth . . ." I gasped.

The mermaid, looking over her shoulder, said:

> *All the tales that sailors tell*
> *Are none so strange as the secret song*
> *The sea lions bark in the dark sea nights*
> *Beneath the crescent moon.*

"What does that mean?" I asked in bewilderment.

Silkie frowned, turned away from the creatures, and said, "Oh, nothing. . . . It's only an old saying. . . . Pay no attention."

When we arrived aboard the *Lizzie Mae*, the mermaid said it was like a great, moving island. She also had never seen rats before and clung tightly to me when a few scurried up to look at her.

"Please, make them go away!" she cried.

I decided to keep her inside the cabin where she wouldn't have to look at them. I filled a little tub with water and put it next to my bed so she could float. And

I sat beside her and told her stories of all the things we would do together when we got home. Sometimes she smiled happily, but at other times there was an anxious look in her eyes. She kept asking how far we had gone from her cove.

That afternoon, as I was at the steering wheel, a huge black cloud slid across the sky and blotted out the sun. The air grew moist; then a thunderous roar filled the heavens, then another and another, and brilliant flashes of lightning appeared. Torrents of rain came pelting down. I went inside to get my raincoat.

Huddled on the bed, the mermaid was peering out of a porthole. She was shivering and seemed terribly frightened. "I have never been in a storm before. I always used to dive under the water or hide in my cave when I saw one coming," she said.

"It will be all right," I assured her.

On deck, all the rats were scurrying about, squeaking loudly. I told them to calm down and get to their stations. Some of them obeyed, but the rest simply ignored me and went on squealing in terror.

Strong winds whipped the sails and caused the ocean to roll and churn. I was thrown against some crates as the ship lurched upward. To and fro we tossed in the howling gale. Then, through sheets of rain, dark shadows loomed ahead—the Bubble Reefs! "Oh, no," I thought. "We'll be dashed to pieces for sure!"

I ran for the wheel, but the wind tore it from its post. One of the masts cracked. The roof of the cabin started to cave in. I rushed inside and grabbed the horrified

mermaid. At this moment she seemed more like a fish than ever. "Oh," she sobbed, clinging to me, "I never should have left my cove! The sea lions were right!"

"I don't understand!" I cried.

"There is a legend that once something has entered the Sea of Spume, it may never leave. That means me . . . and the colored lights and you . . . and this ship!"

"How silly!" I said. "Captain Hoot left. So we can, too."

At that instant, the second mast cracked. Waves rolled over the deck, washing everything into the sea; barrels, crates, and ropes all disappeared. And the rats! Where were the rats? Looking over the rail, I saw all the rats making off in one of the rowboats. They had loaded it with the last of the food and had taken my compass and charts as well. "Come back, you wee traitors!" I screamed.

The third mast cracked, fell, and knocked the cabin to bits! I felt Silkie wiggling in my arms and looked down, only to find that I was holding a small, brown sea lion with dark, wet eyes. Why, she wasn't a mermaid at all! From somewhere a voice (was it Silkie's?) whispered, "All things are as you want them to be in the Sea of Spume." And with a squirm, the little sea lion slipped from my grasp and tumbled over the side of the ship. And as she hit the water, the foam gathered round her head like hair, and she was a mermaid again. The last I saw of her, she was bobbing off to sea, smiling and waving good-bye before diving beneath the waves where she would be safe.

Immediately after that, the ship was hurled upon a reef and destroyed!

The next thing I knew, the storm had abated and I was floating on a calm sea, clutching a piece of board. But the *Lizzie Mae* was gone forever. The mermaid was gone, too. And Captain Hoot's treasure was at the bottom of the deep.

As I drifted in the chill water, alone, hungry, and exhausted, I thought of the rats. They had probably put ashore by now and were feasting on the food they had stolen. The treacherous rodents! If they hadn't panicked, we might have come through the storm safe and sound. It was all their fault, and somehow I would make them pay for it!

After a day or so, some kind fisherman discovered me, and when they saw the condition I was in, they took me to their home on a nearby coast. There I was given plenty of warm food and water and nursed back to health, but I was no longer the same alligator. My spirit had vanished.

Eventually, I wrote to my friends Dirty Mo, Little Quee, and the puffin, to let them know that I was safe, but that I would not be returning to Catfish Bay. I was too ashamed to face all the other sailors and too disgusted with myself. My career as a sailor was over.

I haven't seen my friends since, nor set foot upon the sea. I came to this place because it is where my relatives live. I lead a quiet life and fish alone from the shore. But sometimes on the darkest nights, it seems that the howling wind is the song the sea lions sang there on that lonely ocean.

And so I am as you see me now, in my little shack with the rats treading like trolls across the ceiling, and the shutters knocking at the wind, and the floorboards creaking.

I have been here for a long time.

How the Story Ends

The night after Uncle Tooth's story about the wreck of the *Lizzie Mae*, Corduroy had trouble sleeping. He sat in bed and watched the moonlight cast rippling patterns of trees on the walls of his room. The shadows looked like waves; and when the wind moaned, it made him think of storm-tossed seas and daring quests.

He thought, "It's too bad Uncle Tooth is only remembering *old* adventures instead of having *new* ones. We both seem to be stuck in this dreary place. . . . Well, at least we have each other." And then the wind lulled him to sleep, where he had a deep, soft dream of the sea.

A couple of days later, Corduroy went again to visit

Uncle Tooth. As he approached the shack, he could hear someone singing in a cracked voice:

> With a yo ho hee
> I'll go back to the sea
> With spirit and song
> And voyages long;
> There isn't a happier chap than me!

And there was Uncle Tooth out in the yard. He had unwrapped the boat, had turned it on its side, and was busy making repairs.

Corduroy opened the gate. "Hullo, Uncle Tooth. Whatever are you doing?"

"Ahoy! What does it look like I'm doing? I'm fixing up my ship."

"You mean you . . ." gasped Corduroy.

"Aye, that's it. I'm going to sea again."

Corduroy could hardly believe his ears. Was Uncle Tooth really serious about this? It was all so unexpected that Corduroy had to sit down on the little bench outside the window.

Uncle Tooth wiped his brow, stood up, and fished round in his pockets for his pipe. "Time to take a rest," he said.

He sat on the bench next to Corduroy and lit his pipe. "It's all due to a dream: not a wishful kind of dream, a sleeping dream. I had it the night after I told you my last story."

THE DREAM

I was on my ship, the *Lizzie Mae*, sailing through hazardous waters. The fog was so thick I could barely see the prow ahead of me. Then, out of the mist loomed a dark shadow which looked like another sailing ship. I steered toward it, and as I got closer, an uncomfortable feeling crept over me.

It was a large ship with many mastheads and portholes, but the wood from which it was made was rotten and green. It looked like a deserted pirate ship. Instinct told me that something evil lurked there, but I decided to go aboard anyway and explore.

Securing my own ship so she would not drift off, I tossed up my sturdy rope ladder and ascended.

The deck was deserted, except for several small spiders crawling in and out of holes in the greenish wood.

A purplish moss covered the cabin. All the portholes were cracked and broken, with only a few shards of glass dangling here and there. Rows of ancient cannons lined the sides of the ship. Where the sails used to be, there remained only a few ragged pieces of tarpaulin.

Drawing my cutlass, I thoroughly investigated every foot of the deck, then went into the cabin. It was pitch-black inside, so I lit a match, illuminating several double-decker beds, a trunk, and an old oak desk with the ship's log on it. Looking at the log, I was horrified to see the words YOU'VE HAD YOUR REVENGE, TOOTH. LET US BE!

The match went out. I was attempting to strike a new one when I heard odd skittering sounds behind me. I struck another match and turned round, only to be faced with a ghastly sight: there on the floor of the cabin were dozens and dozens—hundreds—of white rats with small red eyes! They were standing perfectly still, staring at me—and I could see through them! To my horror, I realized that they were ghost-rats, spirits of all the rats I had murdered over the years!

They slowly began to advance toward me. I screamed, dropped my cutlass, and ran on deck. Hurrying down the rope ladder, I jumped into icy water. The *Lizzie Mae* was gone!

Looking up, I saw all the ghost-rats peering over the ship, squeaking and pointing at me. They certainly were angry! Then, out of the fog popped several sea lions. Strings of jewels dangled from their ears, diamond tiaras adorned their heads, and strewn about them in the foamy water were the rubies and emeralds of Captain Hoot's treasure.

"Aroo!" they barked. But this time I could understand them. In hollow voices the sea lions sang:

All who enter the Sea of Spume
Must be prepared to meet their doom.
Once you're in you can't get out;
You're trapped in a watery tomb!

To think I was back in that dreaded sea, the source of all my sorrow! Well, I was determined not to be stuck there, so shouting "That's what you think!" I vigorously swam in the other direction. To my surprise, neither the rats nor the sea lions made any attempt to follow me, and I quickly left them behind. The next thing I knew, I was in the midst of the Bubble Reefs. This time there was no storm to stop me, and I slipped through with no trouble at all. What a relief! I felt that I had finally escaped from the rats and the haunted sea forever. I was free!

Corduroy gave a little jump in his seat. "What a scary dream!" he said.

"Aye," replied Uncle Tooth. "It was an awfully scary dream, but it started me thinking: All this time I thought I had lost my ability as a sailor. It's true, I did lose the *Lizzie Mae* and the treasure and the mermaid— but *I* survived. I am probably the only person who has come out of the Sea of Spume and lived to tell about it. I should have been proud instead of blaming myself all these years and taking it out on the poor rats."

Uncle Tooth paused to re-light his pipe. "I've been living too much with memories. Heck, I ain't so old! Why, in these past twelve years there must be a whole mess of new things just waiting to be explored. Telling you those stories made me realize that sailing is the only type of living I ever cared about or wanted. So I'm going to look up my old friends and resume my career. Lend me a paw, and we'll have this old tub seaworthy in no time!"

All the rest of the week, Corduroy helped Uncle Tooth repair the boat. It was just a middle-sized vessel: not large, not small, but it would do well enough. They sealed the cracks in the side with tar, sanded the mast, sewed patches in the sail where it was ripped, and scraped the barnacles off the hull.

Corduroy worked industriously, happy to be helping his uncle, but it made him sad to think that at the end of the week, the only friend he ever had would sail away forever. But he tried not to dwell on these thoughts. And after eight days of hard labor, there she sat, as proud a little ship as you could ever hope to see.

"Ah, she's a breath of a ship, ain't she?" beamed Uncle Tooth.

"She sure is," replied Corduroy. "What are you going to call her?"

Uncle Tooth, who was just opening a bucket of black paint, said, "I think I'll call her *Courage*. It's a good name, an inspiring name!" And taking a brush, he dipped it into the paint and wrote the ship's name across the prow.

That afternoon, they hoisted the *Courage* onto some long, flat planks of wood and slid her down the rocks to the ocean. Smoothly, the ship slid into the water and bobbed up and down on the waves. Both Corduroy and Uncle Tooth gave a hearty cheer. A golden sunset was brightening the sky, and the whole world seemed waiting.

"Well, I had better start for home now," said Corduroy sadly. "Auntie Hick will miss me at dinner. I'll be back tomorrow morning to see you off."

Uncle Tooth did not turn round. He stood puffing on

his pipe, still full of admiration for the little ship. "Ain't she the loveliest sight?" he said at last. "A dream come true!"

Corduroy started up the cliffs, his head sunk onto his chest. Then he heard Uncle Tooth say, "Oh, by the way, I've been thinking. Isn't it about time you started a life of your own? I mean, you'll never get anyplace stuck here with these dull people."

Corduroy stopped and sighed. "I know, but where can I go?"

Uncle Tooth chewed on his pipe in that thoughtful way. "Well, there is a position for first mate open on my ship. . . ."

"Oh, Uncle Tooth!" cried Corduroy. And they ran and hugged each other.

Early the next day, Corduroy left the stationery shop and Auntie Hick forever. He placed a note on his pillow which said:

> Good-bye. I am leaving with Uncle Tooth
> for a life at sea. Do not worry about me.
> We will take care of one another. I guess
> we are both looney.
>
> Love,
> Corduroy Alligator

He took only his umbrella, a carpetbag filled with his pajamas and toothbrush, and the spyglass Uncle Tooth had given him.

When he got to the shore, the morning sun was rising to announce the new day, the gulls were crying with abandon, and there was his Uncle Tooth waiting by the *Courage,* waving his cap in greeting.

And so they set sail on that fine bright morning, the old alligator who had seen so much, and the young alligator who was seeing it all for the first time. And they sang as they went, because adventure lay before them. They would discover it together and make poems of their own. They were going to find the place where the ocean meets the sky.